"You're not free yet. You're still a very fearful person, and those fears manifest in the people around you. All you can do is listen to that terrible sound of the machete and watch as they burn down the bamboo forest. They sense this when you approach, and they act accordingly. I know what you're thinking. You heard the bridge of dreams breaking, somewhere." She is quiet for a few moments. Then, in a steady voice, she says: *"Nza nja mend tub do nit to?* Can you hold back the sea? The bridge of dreams broke, but this world does not belong to you."

Red Ants

RED ANTS

Pergentino José

translated by Thomas Bunstead

DEEP VELLUM PUBLISHING
DALLAS, TEXAS

Deep Vellum Publishing
3000 Commerce St., Dallas, Texas 75226
deepvellum.org · @deepvellum

Deep Vellum is a 501c3 nonprofit literary arts organization
founded in 2013 with the mission to bring
the world into conversation through literature.

Copyright © Pergentino José, 2012
Originally published as *Hormigas rojas* by Almadía Ediciones,
Oaxaca City, Mexico, 2012
English translation copyright © Thomas Bunstead, 2020

FIRST EDITION, 2020

Support for this publication has been provided in part by grants
from the National Endowment for the Arts, the Texas Commission
on the Arts, the City of Dallas Office of Arts and Culture's
ArtsActivate program, and the Moody Fund for the Arts:

978-1-64605-019-2 (paperback) | 978-1-64605-018-5 (ebook)

LIBRARY OF CONGRESS CONTROL NUMBER: 2020940612

Cover image by Martín Ramirez, "Untitled" (circa early 1950s).
Image used with permission of the Martín Ramirez Estate.

Cover design by Justin Childress | justinchildress.co

Interior Layout and Typesetting by Kirby Gann

PRINTED IN THE UNITED STATES OF AMERICA

CONTENTS

From Inside

I NEED TO FIND LISNIT, I need to get out.
Moss covers the sides of the building. The
ground begins to shake, a few roof tiles fall
to the ground. Moonlight filters in through
the fresh gap, the room growing cold as night
wears on. I hear footsteps up above me somewhere. Two women are talking.

"I told you to stay at home, Cecilia. Who's
going to look after the children, the little one
especially?"

"But Isabel, you don't have any children
that need looking after now. That's why you're
here: you're waiting for the door to open."

"No children—of course I have children!
I went out with the little one on my back just
this morning. I crossed the river, and then I

was coming along the side of the building—
that's when I realized he'd gone."

They speak in hushed tones, seeming not
to want to be overheard.

"Cecilia, wait. I heard someone breathing.
Down there. Hear that? Ragged breaths, like
they're in pain. We have to go down, we have
to find out who it is."

"No way I'm going down there. I need to
wait for my boy, he's bound to come this way."

"You should have thought about that
before you took such risks—the river's been
so high."

"But I had to get him to the doctor, or had
to try at least. The illness, it's begun eating
away at his feet."

Another tremor, lighter this time. Another
beam falls from the roof. The women are quiet
for a moment, before going on:

"Something happened, Cecilia."

"You mean the hospital fire?"

"The hospital fire, yes—why did they
evacuate us like that—why be so hard about

it? They didn't think, not even for a second, about the mothers among us, the fact we live so far away, the chance of the river sweeping us away. First they kill our children, and since then it feels like they've been killing us too. You remember, Cecilia? We come back to Kelobee and no one knows us anymore, it's like we're just shadows. We have to go out at night: the dogs barking at us is the only way to feel like we're alive. I don't know what I'd do without you, Cecilia, don't leave me . . . I think someone's still listening. I can hear the breathing — there, there it is. Ragged breaths — it's like all of Kelobee's pain is in them."

"More like a bull, breathing like that."

I try to calm my breathing, but they can still hear me.

"See, down there. Someone must have been left behind, that must be why they're so agitated."

A large cloud passes in front of the moon, plunging the room into darkness. I hear the voices of the women up above, but I can't understand what they're saying. The cold intensifies, I hear footsteps. The women come nearer, dark shapes in the gloom.

"Sorry," says one. "Is there a way out of here?"

"I don't know," I say. "I've been trapped since nightfall."

"We've been up there, but it's so . . . god-forsaken. We thought we'd come down."

They ask me where I'm from.

"Oh, Kelobee."

"Us too. We were there when the locusts came and devoured the corn crop. We've just heard about the terrible illness there . . ."

"Don't listen to her, mister," says the second woman, cutting her off. "We often come walking around here when the moon's bright, like tonight. But we go home as soon as the sun starts coming up."

I try to imagine what might have brought them here.

"Why is everything shaking?" I ask.

"Such sadness, such suffering," says one.

"The earth shakes when this many people are in pain."

The building is covered in a layer of moss that means the walls are eternally damp. A reddish light begins to unfurl on the horizon. The women whisper to one another. One looks at me and says:

"We're going, it's nearly dawn."

"Where?"

"Wherever our footsteps take us," they answer in unison.

"You can't leave this place," I say. "You need to understand: there's no way out."

The emptiness inside me wishes to continue the conversation, but the women can no longer hear me. They tiptoe over to the worm-eaten door, and one reaches for the handle, but it turns to dust at her touch. In the growing light, objects become clear. One of the women turns and her face is wizened, parched from years of drought. A faint morning breeze blows away the dust, and then the door disappears entirely.

Red Ants

"MAO CHA NZO GO'?" I say—Does anyone live here? but the red ants are busily going about and ignore me. I go down the stairs inside the entranceway, taking my shoes off so as not to make any noise. There's a woman with a fan.

"The people here cast no shadows," she says, "and their footsteps make no sound."

She's right, there's no sound whatsoever. I put my shoes back on. The house is awash with warm air. Someone comes over—a man in a soldier's uniform. What am I doing here, he wants to know.

"Looking for Georgina," I say.

"You have to give me more than that," he says.

"She hasn't been home in two days, her daughter's beside herself."

"Go on," the official says, making a note in a dog-eared logbook. He murmurs something I don't catch, then: "Looking for Georgina, is that it?" He's sneering now. "Lot of problems with the illness this year, more than ever. Come this way, if you'd be so kind."

He holds out a card: it is green and bears a photo of Georgina's face.

"I didn't expect to find a photo of her here," I say.

"I don't know what you're talking about," says the official. "It must be your memory. It's just a card; all I see is a green card."

Soft violin music hangs on the air. A little way off stands a courtyard, with chairs in it and ferns and spiny reeds. The music builds, like the winds of a great hurricane.

"Excuse me," says the official. "Would you have any qualms about coming underground? Down these stairs?"

"Not at all," I say.

The sound of the violin gradually fades.

"First things first. Mind telling me her name again?"

We stop in front of an old computer. The official types, and—alongside a picture of Georgina—my words appear on the screen: "Georgina Navarro. Absent from home for two days. Daughter upset."

The child called out for her mother all night long. I tried to comfort her, speaking in Zapotec, the only language she knew:

"Lo nzind ntio xnii laxio, ya kuand na nza." Which means: We'll look for her in the morning.

There was no one else to comfort the child. She cried, she wanted her mother.

"Ngont nta la," I said. Don't cry.

There is groundwater all around us, and the sound of crows. In the night, hundreds of echoing voices.

"I was worried you'd find me," says Georgina. "Why do you always come looking for me?"

I don't know what to say.

She crouches down and picks a stone up out of a puddle.

"Sometimes you get frightened," she says, "sometimes you tell people your fears . . . I told you to wait for me at the entrance, where the ants are."

"Your daughter's beside herself, she's been crying and asking after you."

"Lubia. Where is she? I haven't seen her for days."

"She was right by the building, she needed to know if you were in here."

Georgina says nothing for a moment, then:

"A mist came in during the afternoon," she says. "Lubia and I were going through the coffee plantation, we were using plastic bags to keep the rain off. You couldn't see but a few feet ahead, and when I turned around the girl had gone. I retraced my steps. The birds were squawking and flapping about in the rain, but Lubia was nowhere to be seen. We'd been picking coffee since morning; we carried on even after it started raining. When the leaves get wet in the country around there, the gnats come swarming up, and god if those little bastards don't bite; pretty soon it's like you're going to explode with the itching. We'd stayed in spite of the rain—the plantation owner had given us the plastic bags—but we planned to leave when it got dark. And Lubia was tired, she was worn out—so much so that I'd made a little bed for her earlier on, clearing away the wet leaves so she could nestle down for a while. My body was starting to vibrate from the itching. Señor Ezequiel had let us have that part of the plantation to ourselves, so I could go out picking with my girl and not worry. He gave her a little basket of her own. 'She's walking now, so she must be eating, yes?' the owner said. 'So she must be strong enough to pick too.' 'Yes, Señor,' I said.

"On our way home, I had the sack of beans, half-full, on my back. I thought Lubia was walking behind me as usual, but, next thing I knew, she wasn't there. Just the sound of the birds. I dropped the sack and went back along the path. I carried on until what light there was, in all that mist, started to fade. The fireflies came out from the wet bushes and plants, and soon it was crane flies coming at me instead of gnats. I shouted for Lubia all through the plantation but got no answer. I walked on alone, and the birds continued making a racket and the rain dripped on me through the trees. It turned to night and I carried on shouting Lubia's name. I went back to Don Ezequiel's house to tell him. The old man was warming himself by the wood burner. 'That's kids for you,' he said. 'She'll be out there somewhere playing.' 'No, Señor, that can't be. I looked and looked, I looked until it was really dark.'"

Now I interrupt:

"All this about Lubia," I say. "But what about me?"

Georgina looks down. She turns and walks, unhurriedly, back along the underground paths. The violin music, so tranquil, begins again. As though that were Georgina's answer. In the distance, in the courtyard with the chairs, ferns, and reeds, the red ants go on working. So busy, nothing else registers with them.

Threads of Steam

I'M IN A CELL NEXT to a boiler room. Steam rises up past me, escaping through a broken window above. It is stiflingly hot—my hair feels singed. Then I find that a pair of men, both bald, are approaching. One hands me a piece of paper: "You've been sent this," he rasps. "From out there."

I unfold it and, incredibly, find words written by Itza—her handwriting. A couple of lines, no more. I try to stay calm enough to read them. "If these words could be of any use, it would be as a reminder, however slight . . ." There is more, but the writing after that isn't legible.

The second guard—the heavier of the two—booms:

"Walk."

We come down a damp wooden stairwell. I wish I had time to understand what
Itza meant—however partially. What joins
her to me, me to her? It has only been a few
days and the memory of her has all but faded.
Her eyes half-closed, as if hiding something:
this is the sensation my imprisonment pro-
vokes. The outside world, how quickly it
fades. The rickety stairwell descends a long
way, until finally we reach the bottom, entering a low hallway—I have to duck. The floor
is covered in water. As I take forward steps,
it becomes apparent just how deep the water
is, and how fast-flowing. My legs begin to
shake, and yet I avoid letting on that I'm
afraid. Up ahead, where the water is coming from, I see the tall flame of a very large
candle. Then the water sweeps the fat guard
off his feet and carries him away, but after a
few meters he manages to grab on to a thick
piece of rope fastened at either side of the
channel. He is battered head-on by the water

until, gathering all my strength, I take hold of his arm and drag him over to the levee wall. Staggering under the weight of him, I end up near the wooden table where the lit candle stands. Beyond it, in a dark room, a glimpse of flickering votives. The water slaps loudly against something, some nook in the building we have reached. The guard, exhausted and gripping my shoulder, drags his feet as we come through into the candlelit room. A sudden calm comes over me — the very calm I have been trying to attain for days . . . What is this place? The closer we get, the more keenly I want to know: what is inside?

There is the smell of brackish water. Low light — my eyes adjust only gradually. I hear a shrill voice chanting something ritualistic and for a few seconds single this out in my hearing; foreign words, unfamiliar and beautiful. I move slowly nearer — trying to work out what mysterious function this room serves. Candles of every size have been set out in circles, and a number of them have burned down to stubs.

I realize a photograph has been placed in the center. The ceremonial chant is still filtering in from somewhere. Then, with a shudder, I see that it's my mother in the photo: sitting on a bench in an empty park, a youthful look in her eyes, she appears to be trying to decipher whatever it is she's looking at. I move closer: her hair, unmistakably hers, is shoulder-length. I am reminded of the threads of steam coming from the boiler, the warm, eddying air; our faces being spat on; and the morning we were marched around the building's central patio . . .

A voice shouting orders, and only some of us able to walk after being forced to walk over broken glass. I saw two old men fall down. The spindly guard, black wool hat on his head, hobbled along giving orders.

"Quick march, you lumps! Hup, hup, hup-two-three-four!"

The early dawn was intensely cold, and those of us who could still walk were soaked through after the previous night's downpour.

An old officer, his winter coat wrapped snugly around him and a malicious smile on his face, amused himself by saluting anyone who was about to fall down; he would lean in and say a few words, though by that point I could barely understand anything . . .

Inside the candlelit room, hot air seems to spring up from the corners, clouding our vision. The pain subsides a little as the air thins and grows a little cooler, and yet when we start trying to breathe it in, we realize we cannot. We lose our bearings. All this steam.

"Stay together, comrades," says a voice.

I stay calm. I know there is someone, somewhere, who could call this whole charade to an end at any moment. Something behind that malicious smile, I just know it. An image appears in my thoughts and settles there: I see my mother in conversation with an old, kind-looking man. I have the sense that he and my mother used to talk together sometimes. Maybe he knew who I was, and it was he who broke the rules and returned the photo to me—it was taken from me before they placed me in this cell.

The air is suffocating. I feel the steam collecting behind my earlobes and laying wet on my hair. I don't know the location of the park in the photograph, or the occasion, or why the old man at the entrance decided to let me have it. How might my mother have known him? It's two years since I've seen her. She used to like going for long walks at night, going out to the deserted city limits.

She was the first person to mention the existence of the Rastras to me. They used to meet not far from where we lived, and I soon became obsessed with finding out who they were. I should not have allowed myself to become so curious, much less to let myself get sucked into that group of kidnappers in the city. We used to pose as a company selling padlocks and had a simple method for drawing our victims in: inviting people to interview for jobs abroad. We were discreet; it never came to physical violence. I did not imagine our own boss could also allow those working for him to be abducted.

We had one rule: never to look our potential victims in the eye. But this small pleasure was one I allowed myself. It was all hidden in there, the sadness of some, the indifference of others. They would merely ask what the work entailed, and were only too happy to give an account of their technical abilities. They were not inclined to speak about anything other than themselves, nor did they have the time. One person a week. We were careful not to get caught, and the levels of unemployment in the city played into our hands. The people came right to us—to our offices. Registered offices, I ought to point out—aboveboard, all taxes paid.

A glance in the eye of an interviewee was enough to tell me if they were a good candidate. Our boss would inform those we had chosen that their technical abilities meant they were being sent to one of the company's branches abroad, where the work was more challenging. But I knew they would never see their homes again.

How would my mother feel if she saw me now, choking on this corrosive steam? The guard isn't here anymore, he's gone. My energies are fading — I feel like lying down and sleeping. I walk to the end of the room and all the way back, through thick, billowing steam. All that remains is for fate to run its course.

Then, through the heat, I feel a sharp blast of cold on one of my knees. A burning, toxic stab expands inside me, spilling flecks of light across my field of vision. Suddenly I see my mother before me, walking through the steam. Her face is contorted — as though in overwhelming pain. I feel myself begin to fall but manage to keep to my feet. I think of Itza, the one memory I can grasp on to. My mother walks toward an iron door at the far end of the room, it seems to be the way out. I remember the time Itza came to our house at dawn one day after an argument with her father. My mother knocks on the door and disappears through it. I walk over, my feet sliding on the wet floor—but find it won't open. I kneel, as in some simple prayer, begging it to open. The room falls silent, and the steam grows denser still. The door won't open. I try to think of Itza, only for lights to explode inside my mind.

Room of Worms

A BOY IS CRYING: I am enveloped by his lament. Next to a lit candle, near the boy, a worm wriggles along. Worms are falling from the ceiling; so consumed with sorrow is the boy, he doesn't seem to notice. I am sitting near him and I have the sensation of being watched. The worms are yellowish in color.

"Let's get out of here," I say to the boy.

"No," he says. "I'm waiting for my mom."

"Come on."

"No," he says through his tears. "I have to wait for her."

"Come on," I say, trying to pick him up. "Look at all these cockroaches and worms, they're everywhere."

"I have to wait for her, she might come

back at first light. It's still dark out there. Did you bring the candle?"

"It was already here in the room," I say. "I just lit it."

We hear footsteps approaching. The worms continue to rain down.

"I thought she'd be here," says the boy, his gaze intense as we watch the falling worms. "She's been gone a long time. Our house is nearby. I was playing in the hallway last night, and I thought my mom was doing her knitting as usual. None of my friends were around, and I walked to the lake, and I threw stones there for a while, until it started getting dark. I went home but my mom still wasn't there. I thought she'd come here."

I tell the boy to be careful not to blow out the candle; it's the only light in the whole house.

"Let's get out of here," I insist. "These worms are horrible, they're all over my clothes."

"What are you here for?" he says, ignoring my request.

"I'm looking for a friend of mine, a girl I haven't seen in a very long time. Someone said I should come and look for her here."

"I'll help you find her," says the boy. "Once I've found my mom."

More footsteps out in the hallway, but nobody comes to the door. Nobody comes into the room.

I was picking my way between bamboo plants when I heard someone say in Zapotec that the bridge of dreams is broken. And then:

"Nza nja mend ntub do nit to." It's like trying to hold back the sea.

This was followed by the sound of a crowd sweeping through the forest, the murmur of people moving closer, *ñee mend mbchas mbii mend*, as though they were floating on the air. And the sound of machetes, and laughter. Birds calling, wings flapping, startled butterflies taking to the air; something was going on. The spider webs on the bamboo plants had

been torn down, along with the bamboo itself.
Coming along the path, I hear that same voice
again:

"Nza nja mend ntub do nit to."

I begin to make out what the people are
saying.

"Keep cutting! Quick! We need to get
through it all before the owner gets back.
Bamboo? Get rid of it, he says! He wants coffee plants, nothing but coffee plants. We'll get
a bigger crew if we need to. People are flaky,
you tell them it needs doing by a certain day,
and do they do it by then? Bamboo produces
nothing—moths eat right through it."

It is a good thing to go walking in the
forest, when you are free to do so. The bamboo leaves are like paper. They form a canopy
overhead. I remember talking to a boy a number of days ago, in a room where worms rained
down from the ceiling. I heard the bridge of
dreams breaking, somewhere.

•

My friend is inside a dark building. I ask her to turn the lights on.

"What light?" she says. "It's daylight or nothing here. It's gotten late now—didn't you notice it getting late?"

We drink tea and talk in the half-light.

"Why are you here?" I ask.

"This room has been here for a long time," she says.

We see cockroaches and worms moving across the floor. She opens a window to let in the scant evening light; night is already falling. The boy is also with us, and he interrupts.

"He," he says, pointing at me, "he told me he'd help me out of here."

He has an innocent face—he must be about four years old. I told his mother we were together in the room of worms.

My friend says, "You are free when you walk in the bamboo forest. There are butterflies, flowers, and the wind moves around you so silently."

"But there's the sound of machetes," I tell her. "People are chopping down the forest. They've even got children cutting the bamboo down."

"How do you know?" she asks.

"I brought this," I say, and I show her a bamboo shoot, freshly cut.

It's daytime, which is why I can hear the birds flapping and screeching. My friend asked me to come and find her in this building, but I don't know what I'm doing creeping forward so quietly between the bamboo plants. I think about the room of worms. I see vines and enormous butterflies. "*Mplo nda go'?*" a man asks me. He is sitting beneath a bamboo plant, smoking. Where are you going? A dog barks. There are other men at work, and they look at me uncertainly, grasping their machetes.

"Can I go this way?" I ask.

The man smoking gets up, comes a few steps nearer and says, "No. This is Don Elpidio Alonso's plantation."

"I see. Is there a path I'm allowed to go on?"

He breathes out a large lungful of smoke.

"We've been working for days. The owner hasn't paid us. He hasn't been home in quite some time, but here we are, we go on cutting the bamboo. We have to make the most of the rain—until the blue jays sing in happiness at all the water."

"Why are you cutting down the bamboo forest?"

"So coffee can be grown instead. The owner will be back any day. When we go up to the big house they say, 'He'll be here soon, he'll be here soon.'"

It's almost midday. These men won't let me pass. But I hear footsteps. It sounds like large numbers of people approaching, *ñee mend mbchas mbii mend*, as though they are floating on the air. They come to the clearing and begin hacking at the straight, yellow stalks with their machetes. The erratic fluttering of the butterflies is a reflection of what is going on.

Many hands bringing down the forest.

"You're better off not trying, mister," says a woman with a boy strapped to her back, as she continues hacking at the bamboo. "You'll only get lost. There's only one path across this forest."

My friend and I listen as people talk in the courtyard outside.

"They're saying the owner's coming," she concludes.

I go over to the window and look out at the people.

"Seems the owner's unhappy," says my friend, pacing the room.

"You tricked me," I say eventually. "The forest is being torn down, and you knew it was; you've lived here longer than me. I don't know why you asked me to come and look for you here. You said that when a person is free, they're at liberty to go walking in the forest, but there are people out there cutting down trees, and no one's stopping them. And you've got your child with you—it's dangerous for him. I tried to get across the forest this morning and they wouldn't let me. I don't think we'll find a way."

She sits down near the window and is quiet for a time, takes slow breaths. Then she answers.

"You're not free yet. You're still a very fearful person, and those fears manifest in the people around you. All you can do is listen to that terrible sound of the machete and watch as they burn down the bamboo forest. They sense this when you approach, and they act accordingly. I know what you're thinking. You heard the bridge of dreams breaking, somewhere." She is quiet for a few moments. Then, in a steady voice, she says: "*Nza nja mend tub ∂o nit to?* Can you hold back the sea? The bridge of dreams broke, but this world does not belong to you."

Outside the people are shouting, "The owner's arrived! Don Elpidio Alonso's here!"

The light in the room begins to dwindle. I hear my friend go out. She opens the door, and a fragile layer of light reaches into the house. Shutting the door behind her, she walks away into the bamboo forest.

Not to You

IT WAS A CLOUDY AFTERNOON; something ominous in the air. Two men in purple masks addressed me, almost in unison and enunciating their words with great care:

"It's Genoveva we are looking for, not you. We know she isn't in at your house, but she'll be going back to school very soon and we've come to tell you you're never going to see her again."

They tried to speak simultaneously, no easy thing. Their speech delivered, they seemed disquieted. The masks covered their faces. They stood in silence and I knew they were hiding something else.

My feet felt planted in the ground. In the land around us stood encino trees, with dried vines hanging from their branches. Dense clouds crashed into the mountainsides. The air was freezing. I tried to speak, but my mind was all of a jumble. The way they peered at me, the two men, it was as if they were trying to record my every expression. Then one of them, for no apparent reason, prostrated himself before me, kneeling with arms outstretched. His mask flat to the ground.

"We've been sent to warn you. It's true. Yesterday, when you watched your daughter come home and take off her checkered uni-form, as always—that was the last time you'll ever do so. Do you understand?"

I stood very still, listening. I could not move even my pinkies. I tried blinking but my eyelids took an age to respond. The wild-eyed man was speaking more loudly now. His mask was streaked with soil. The mist was so low it had all but enveloped us.

"Go back to your home. You need to accept that you're never going to see Genoveva again. Our need of her outweighs yours. We have come to thank you for the precious gift that is your girl. We want to ask you not to cry for her. Not only will your tears serve no purpose, they will make her feel sad when she joins us, and we won't know how to console her."

The voice coming from behind that purple mask disgusted me; the other man simply watched his partner. The one with the wild eyes went prattling on:

"Go home, that's all, and tell your mother, she who has cared for your daughter since birth, that you and your wife took her, that you are unable to understand her dreams. Tell her you took the train last night on a whim, to Roatina, where your daughter's mother lives. That's what you'll say, don't forget: you went up the wooden steps, you knocked, her mother came out in her dressing gown, you handed the girl over and got straight back on the train, arriving just before nightfall. Tell this to your mother: Genoveva isn't going to be with us anymore. At first, she won't be able to accept it, but she'll get used to it in the end."

As he spoke, he carried on touching his face to the ground, or hitting it—harder and harder as he went on, as if this would justify his words. He could hardly breathe. The purple mask was brown with mud by the time he got up. I tried to speak again, but my mouth felt wooden, like I was a mute doll stuck out on this lonely path. The other man raised his hands to the sky and said, "You should go now. Don't stray from the path, and don't think about Genoveva."

His tone was measured. Like a father affectionately instructing a child—placing a hand on my shoulder. Behind the mask, his eyes were brown and he kept blinking, as though to emphasize his words.

For a few moments I was aware of his breathing. I lifted my gaze, looking up beyond the cloudy peaks, and felt my feet moving once more. I could walk again. I wished for it all to have been a bad dream. But no. The clouds, the smell of the grass, the cold of late afternoon, and the men — all were as they had been.

"You have to go home," he said, gazing at me intently. "Tell your mother."

The last rays of sunlight blended with the thick mist, which drew forward over the path, the only way to the village.

I walked along the path, lined with ferns and wild grasses still wet from the afternoon rains. I wanted to get my thoughts in order before I reached the village where I live with my mother and daughter. It started growing dark; I could barely see where I was placing my feet. When I reached Capulín Hill, the village was shrouded in mist. Before I reached Roatina Road, the only paved thoroughfare, I came upon Don Aparicio. He had a waterproof jacket on, and a small cigar dangled from his lips.

"Why the hurry, young man?"

"I have to get back," I said.

"Young people today!" he said, letting out

a booming laugh. "It's good to toughen yourself up in every type of weather!"

As soon as I was underway again, I heard the first bells chime. Others soon joined in, tolling more slowly, and the darkness of the night seemed to muffle them, while the mist seemed to scatter them. Farther on, Don Aparicio caught up with me. He was an old friend of my father's, the two of them would get together sometimes.

"Why the hurry, young man?"

I carried on listening to the bells. I could hardly make out Don Aparicio's face, but his brown eyes brought to mind those of the masked man. The last bell chimed, and Don Aparicio removed his hat. He held out one of his cigars, offering it to me.

"You need to be on your guard, young man."

He hurried ahead of me along the final stretch of the paved road.

The cigar was warm from the old man's hand. It was coffee-colored and flecked with small pieces of mud.

I hurried on as quickly as my legs would carry me. Genoveva was on the swing beneath the leafy guava tree outside the house, swinging back and forth. Her school uniform was muddy. She saw me and rushed over for a shoulder ride.

"When are those women in the house going to leave, Papa?"

Her cheeks were icy cold and her hair was dirty. Then my mother appeared. She was wearing a black dress.

"I've been looking for you all afternoon," she said, looking at the two of us. "Where were you?"

"The bells, why were they ringing the bells?" Then, before she could answer, I said, "Why are those women in the house?"

"A man came looking for you this morning, as soon as you left. He seemed very tired. He said he used to know you and that he would wait for you to get back, however long it was going to take. He said he had been walking for many hours and was cold. We made a place for him to sit near the fireplace. I went into the kitchen to make some tea and when I came back the man was lying on the floor. I looked closer and found he'd stopped breathing. I called the neighbors. They're inside."

My mother took a creased, stained piece of paper from her apron pocket. A name written on it: Jorge Velares Antonio. The handwriting was my own, but I could not remember having written it.

The prayers went on until midnight, but finally tiredness overcame us all. I woke before dawn. The dead man wasn't there anymore. Just the candles and the smell of incense. Where he had lain Genoveva now lay, candles and bunches of white flowers all around her.

Departure

SILENTLY I FLEE. THE JOURNEY is long
and my hopes begin to fade. I am suddenly
taken by a thought, something I feel I must
urgently do: take up position in the window,
shoulder the rifle, gun down the first person
I see coming along the street. An old man, a
businessman with a briefcase—it makes no
difference. I find myself enthused at the prospect of it being some company man, his head
full of money and schemes. How curious it
would be to become an agent of fate, to take
out a stranger with his briefcase in hand, to
put a bullet in him from your window.

Then the police would come. Maybe your
neighbors would see the shot being fired. The
idea that a couple of armed policemen, or

a whole group of them, show up and try to detain me and maybe beat me—it is all part of my plan. What would be awful is if no one saw me take the shot. I also like the idea of shooting down some old man as he comes out of the bakery opposite, bag of bread under his arm. A crowd would gather around, all wanting to glimpse his final breaths. The blood-spattered sidewalk. Maybe an ambulance gets there before the police. People watching as he mumbles a few words and then subsides, the bread rolls sopping red from the blood gushing out of his head.

What would be terrible is if no one were to realize where the deadeye shot came from. Sad, if the news were not to reach every last member of his family. Then he would have died merely because some lunatic felt the need to provoke the world—getting up onto a low bench, taking aim at the first mortal he saw coming along, squeezing the trigger.

What a disgrace if, after it all, no one knocked on my door, no one came and accused me. Say if they arrested the wrong person, or even a couple of people. All because a man like me had decided to take a potshot from his window, like he was out on a duck hunt.

This is my situation. It's time to do something about it. I pour myself a glass of water, begin pacing the room with bare feet. The water goes straight to my stomach, and I remember I haven't eaten since yesterday. I crouch down by the bed, reach underneath it and pull out the wooden gun case. I run my fingers across its cold metal. I cradle it in my arm, put my right eye up to its sights. I level it at the wall, training the crosshairs on the dusty, sea-blue wall.

This color, viewed through the sights, brings me back to earth. I get up onto the small bench I've placed beneath the window.

I look at the clock on the wall. 7:09 a.m. People crowd along the sidewalk. So many lives out there, getting up, going out, hurrying down a street. A simple detail that, to me, seems magical.

A nurse wearing a bonnet, umbrella under her arm, walks quickly along. I guess her to be somewhere in her thirties. Nobody knows I'm here, looking down. A boy in a white sweater and a yellow scarf so thick he can barely breathe is holding a woman's hand as they go along—she fairly drags him. Perhaps she's his mother. The boy, six years old or so, looks half asleep as he stares across at a churros stall. The mother leans down to say something. Sad—it's sad that I could never shoot a boy. I need to act now, before everything I see softens me, softens the things I've been coolly constructing over these stormy nights. The end is approaching. I must not waver. Where have they gone, those madding dreams? When I even went so far as to plunge my feet into cold water to stop myself from going mad, when I would hardly have managed to close my eyes by the time the sun was coming up . . .

Something holds me back. I'm at a loss. I look through the rifle sights and the nurse comes into view. I scan her face close-up. On such cold, stormy nights, I felt the sun would never rise. Something had broken inside me, but I had no idea what.

I'd barely have closed my eyes when an image would come into my head: a menacing flock of crows coming toward me, cawing, bloodthirsty. I would always wake just in time, just as they were about to devour me. Is it too much, cutting short the life of another mortal? I don't know what Nayeli will think when she comes back and sees the bloody mess on the sidewalk outside . . . The image of the crows returns. They rain down on me. The first time the nightmare has come to me while I am awake. The room full of them. Everywhere, they darken everything. The air a churning mass of dark wings, those hateful eyes.

I take up the rifle again and go over to the window. I see the old man at the churros stand serving some children. Crows are flying in past me, they beat their wings, fill the apartment with beating wings. I shoot. But it's like nothing's happened, nothing but the recoil in my hands. It's like this was the signal they were waiting for: they begin pecking at my back, tearing at my clothes, my skin. The pain spreads across my entire body, until I am knocked down by the beating wings, the cawing. I realize I've pulled the trigger again, and again; I know because of the repeated recoil. The cawing is incessant and grows shriller, sharper—like the birds are trying to communicate with me. The pain becomes more than I can take. I'm on the floor. I see black dots swirling. Pain courses through me. The black dots become many colors, exploding over my eyes before, finally, my vision falls dark.

Heart of Birds

THERE WERE BIRDS EVERYWHERE, plumage red and blue and many different greens. Their screeching resounded among the parched vines that hung down from the branches of the macahuite. It was midday and a voice told me to stay where I was, not far from a rocky ravine, in the shade of these trees. A number of birds—recently hatched herons, from the look of them—began flying around in circles before entering this tangle of dry vines. When they emerged on the far side they had turned into very large birds with immense, dark wings. They flew between the treetops emitting a magpie-like cawing.

I had to be on my guard. I had promised

to care for these birds and would do what I could to keep my word.

Then suddenly I heard a whistling far away—it grew louder and began echoing between vines and ravine. It was as though the sound had woken me from a dream: only now did I realize where I was. The ravine was shot through with mole tunnels. After walking a short distance, I slipped and fell; looking up, I found I was next to a large rock that had been rolled across the entrance to a cave. The stench of rotting flesh hit me. I had begun getting to my feet when I heard voices, people approaching. I hid just inside the cave mouth. An old man with long hair stopped a meter or two from where I was. His face was covered in large scars and he was glancing wildly around. He had a small boy by the hand—the child was struggling to traverse the uneven ground. The noise of the birds grew deafening. With a wry smile, the old man tried to say something in the boy's ear; the boy looked frightened as the birds continued to circle menacingly overhead.

Then the old man, leaning on his stick, let go of the boy's hand and began walking away; when the boy tried to run, he lost his footing and fell, not far from where I stood. I looked around for the old man, but he had disappeared. I picked up some stones and threw them at the birds, which had begun attacking the boy. A dark-winged bird had managed to tear off one of his ears in its beak; I hit the creature and it let go. There was a great clamor of beating wings, and the birds departed.

We were alone for a time, before suddenly my vision filled with shadows: enormous white vultures, their beaks as sharp as great thorns, came and settled in the parched branches of a madroño tree outside the cave mouth. They gazed down at me and the boy in my arms. A single cry came from the largest of the birds, and they all flew away through the treetops. I made the most of the commotion to steal into the cave, taking the boy with me. Inside, I felt something crunching underfoot; I was walking over strange gray shells of some kind, and each time one broke it gave off a foul smell. The cave narrowed as we went farther in. I stumbled on, until eventually emerging into sunlight again: a harsh midday sun.

I heard people arguing loudly in the distance. I caught sight of two young men with machetes coming our way, and when they saw us, they broke into a run. I saw fear in their eyes as they drew nearer. "You are the chosen one!" they said, in near unison.

One of them threw down his machete and knelt. "You have to help us," he implored.

The other followed suit. "We're in trouble," he hissed.

I didn't understand. I watched as one screwed his eyes shut, as though praying with all his might.

I wanted to leave, get away from them, but the one still standing placed his hands on my shoulders and looked me in the eye. "The vultures, we mean. It's your eyes, they're completely white. Just like the king vulture."

"You have to help us," said the other in

a prayerful tone, getting up. "You've come through the vulture cave. They've been gorging themselves on our children. Your feet are covered in the yolks of vulture eggs, which means you've walked through their nests, and you came out completely unscathed. You are the chosen one!"

"I don't understand," I said. "If I was watching the birds all morning, it's only because a voice told me to. I don't recall when, but it said I must one day take care of the forest birds."

"You haven't killed any vultures," said one, "but you have destroyed their eggs."

They took me by the arm and led me along an earthen path. We came to a place where a number of men were sweeping the ground, using large monstera leaves. One of them wore a tattered hat fashioned from palm fronds and had the look of a criminal. Wiping his brow, he said to me, "It's a little farther on, the real problem."

We went on. The pair seemed afraid,

their breathing shallow. Then we came in sight of a huge bull, and when our scent reached it, it began to foam at the mouth, it raked the ground with its hooves. It charged, but I felt a deep sense of peace and made no attempt to run; it ignored me, chasing after my captors instead. Snorting, it knocked one of them down and trampled him. Then I picked up the boy, who had been holding my hand the whole time, and carried him into the long shadow of a macahuite. I put him down and piled dry leaves over him. Something told me the men who had been sweeping the entrance to the path would come and claim him as theirs. The others' astonishment—at the fact I had rescued him—began to make sense. I tried to provoke the bull by running near to it, but it wasn't me it seemed to want. I could hear its breathing. The men with their large monstera leaves came and surrounded the creature, moved in on it and eventually succeeded in forcing it to the ground. Within moments its throat had been slit, and they began gathering its blood in dusty iron pails; the smell of the bull wafted up. The men, intent on skinning the beast, did not notice me; not feeling brave enough to take them on, I went back for the boy.

My mind fell dark: a deep sadness came over me at having failed to help the birds. The sickening smell of the eggs melded with that of the freshly spilt blood of the bull. These details seemed to sharpen my sense of guilt. I remembered what my grandfather used to say: vultures are the dimming of the spirit. Maybe it was he who came to me in my dream a few days ago, he who asked me to protect the birds. I heard his voice once more; the dream was still a mystery to me. I asked myself what my grandfather would have made of me walking over the eggs of vultures, of the fact I had crushed them underfoot. The men didn't seem to see me, so focused were they on the bull hide; they were wrenching apart bones and joints, and blood flowed freely. They were also in some hurry, murmuring to one another, glancing all around, like they were running from something.

Many died that day, a great many, I said to myself in a low voice, over and over, trying to feel less alone, less lost. I heard my grandfather's voice again, it had crept up on me: "Jacobo, the vultures are sacred, you must never throw stones at them."

The words repeated in my mind like a litany.

"Yes, Grandfather, I know. You've told me many times. But today, it was out of my hands."

I look for some path home, feeling my way. I move forward as though inside a dark room, though the sun streams down still.

Prayers

I DECIDE TO GO BACK to the cobblestone
road. The wildflowers that cover the old
facades keep coming back, like weeds. I test
the air for any scent of the man. The same
misshapen rock is there, in the place where I
came across him, sitting there with that blood-
soaked hammer in his left hand. A fierce look
in his eye then as he tried to get up from the
rock—but wasn't able to. I helped him, and
no sooner was he on his feet than he placed
the hammer in my right hand, the blood on it
still warm, still sticky. I realized then that he
was far older than I'd thought, and saw myself
reflected in his unsteadiness. The look in his
eyes—patience, shock, and something else,
something I could not comprehend—is hazy

in my memory. I heard him say, "Forgive me. Lately my mind has been elsewhere."

And, in no hurry whatsoever, he sauntered away down the same cobblestones.

I walk to the end of the road. The silence deepens. I strain to listen, to see if I can make out any sounds. I have crossed half the city, felt impelled to do so in spite of the repeat calls expressly forbidding us from going outside after seven in the evening. The final part of the journey—which brought me here, to the south side of the city, to this road with its abandoned, weed-shrouded buildings—I had to complete on foot. The last rays of sunlight are extinguished. I hear a couple of voices approaching. Two women, talking quietly, whispering almost. My presence startles them, like I've just stepped out of a sewer. The younger-looking one has her head and shoulders partially covered with a blue shawl. She takes a white envelope from a small black bag and holds it out: it's an invitation to a party two blocks from here, she explains. She speaks in a whisper, almost impossible to hear. The other woman, who, judging by the wrinkles visible beneath her thick makeup, could be the first woman's mother, says they're meeting the other partygoers there.

Night is coming down. Though I can barely make out the younger woman's features, she seems wary. In addition to the shawl she wears several white necklaces, giving her a certain elegance. She says, "We never thought Padre Edgardo would rule the city like this. He shut down the two cotton factories, so many people have been cast into poverty, and to top it off we aren't even allowed to walk the streets at this sort of hour."

The other woman nods along to the complaints. I pretend I have to go, telling them I'm just looking for a friend who lives at the end of the street.

"Just along here," I say, hoping they might confirm it for me. "Number 56, Calle Padre Edgardo . . ."

"Listen to the radio," says the older

woman. Her tone is that of a mother imploring her children not to go out into the streets while a terrible event is unfolding. Then the other one, who seems more perturbed still, asks, "Can you read?"

I say I can. Their talk is grating on me, I want to get away now. They're right, it's risky going out walking, but it's my choice. The younger woman exclaims: "Read the newspaper! Every day there's new things. Roads with new names. A new set of people arrested overnight. Buildings seized. People they're going to deport."

Then, as I am beginning to despair, the ceremonial sound of bells strikes up in the distance. The women get down on their knees and start exhorting me in trembling voices. "Read the newspaper, young man," the older woman says. "Do it for Padre Edgardo." And she takes a newspaper from her bag and hands it to me before the pair turn and hurry away, no goodbye—as though the Sentinels were training their sights on them already.

They go off down the paved street, cowering, until I lose sight of them. The last bells chime. They struck fourteen yesterday, I'm sure of it, though my mother insisted it was only thirteen. Then I hear the sirens: the Sentinels' trucks have been deployed. I picture them in their white habits, out to catch any nonconformist during this time of Padre Edgardo's rule. There is something beautiful about this tumult of sirens, the way it breaks over the city: the opening canticles of a ceremony due to last until dawn.

Night has fallen completely, no more light.

The prospect of finding the man with the bloody hammer impels me. That the Sentinels might get to him first, might arrest him, feels unacceptable to me. I feel bad for leaving my mother on her own—with the terrible earache she's had. I've been keeping her going using stolen hospital medicines. It's becoming more than I can bear. I have been unable to gather my thoughts sufficiently to come up with any better way of tracking down the man with the hammer. In my mind he is a kind of hero, a silent drifter through streets, eliminating Sentinels as he goes. I am thrilled by the idea of him, night after night, one by one, taking them out. It has occurred to me that perhaps there are more than one of him: a silent army working in the shadows—one in which I would be only too happy to enlist. It would be difficult to leave my mother, but if the chance arose, I know exactly what I would do. Or perhaps not. When I think of it, I am overcome by such doubt, such uncertainty— it makes me feel like giving up. Some nights they fail to catch anyone out on the streets, and so enter people's homes instead and snatch them, thus reaffirming their loyalty to Edgardo. One of the effects is that, for a long while, many people have simply stopped thinking: the abandonment of the city center, the factory closures; people are barely shocked. I myself sometimes forget to think about my mother, the terrible pain in her ears.

A gringo doctor took over the running of the hospital two weeks ago. A notice went up listing the illnesses he will not be treating, and earache was near the top. I've had to spend hours down at the warehouse convincing the man in charge that I have a chronic cough, so that I can then swap that medicine for the ones my mother needs.

Keeping her alive has taken more time than I expected, the pain is worse around dawn, as though pricked in some mysterious way by the light. Then the bells chime, telling us we can go out again. My mother, her eyes shining, still submerged in the pain, repeats prayer after prayer—following the list of matins recommended by Edgardo. As if that were all it was—just a recommendation. But these are the prayers that have taken root most easily in Ciudad Pirlo, as it was dubbed a few weeks back.

People stop whatever they are doing and congregate downtown to pray—it's like some kind of epidemic. Or as though they have found something in these prayers that enables them to be free, or at least to breathe.

My mother finishes her prayers, and it's a number of seconds before she will realize what I am doing, watching passersby out the window: young and old, men and women, all together, as though they like going out at such an hour just to attend those prayer sessions at government headquarters. They do not even bother to wait for the bus provided by the government. I see boys in thick coats, old men barely able to put one foot in front of the other. My mother looks at me and says, "A cold day to go praying."

Like dust, the cold has invaded the entire city. People try to blend in with the crowd taking part in the repeat prayer sessions. The format is simple: first they pray for Edgardo, then for all the children, and, next, anyone who wants to may take the floor. This way, people feel part of the ceremonies. They are allowed to pray for anything they like. Women praying for the return of lost dogs has become increasingly common.

I carry on looking out the window. Some people know they won't make it as far as the prayers, but they walk patiently on, as if there was all the time in the world. My mother turns on her bedside radio and we listen to a crackly broadcast of the day's prayers. I go over and change the station. From today on, Edgardo will begin convincing us of the goodness of his rule over the airwaves. Some stations broadcast the prayers yesterday, my mother says. Might the man with the hammer — or the many people who are the man with the hammer — go to the session and ask forgiveness for the murders just committed?

Témpano

THE SMELL OF SILENCE GREW stronger. A silence that the heart cannot ignore. I waited patiently for some human voice that might mark the outer limits of this place for me, and of the cursed hallucinations afflicting the townspeople of La Encrucijada. The outer ring of the town was a line of cobwebbed windows. Two women came over to where I was sitting, and one said, "Are you looking for someone?"

"Elena," I said. "I promised I'd be here before nightfall."

She let out a shrill laugh, while the other woman tried to embrace me, as if she could feel my pain. "I understand you, believe me, I understand you."

"Do you know Elena?" I quickly said.

"No, I don't, but I'd like to meet her. I see great hope in your eyes. You must wait for her; she's sure to come."

The first woman was wearing a halter top, her hair was down, and she smelled strongly of perfume. She seemed unable to keep quiet, and kept murmuring to herself, "Elena, Elena, now they just want to find Elena."

She came up and tried to kiss me, saying, "I'm Elena."

"No!" I said. "You don't even sound like her."

"I am," she said frantically. "I'm Elena." But after a moment she gave up. "Alright, I was wrong, I see it now. You tell me what my name is, then."

"Dolores. Maybe your mother or your grandmother wanted to call you Elena, but your father had his way. Dolores. Do you see now?"

My words seemed to calm her, and she loosened her grip on my hands.

"Fine!" she said in a firm voice. "Elena's coming, I assure you."

And the women went away again, disappearing into the early evening shadows as the seven o'clock train came by, whistle blowing.

Seven o'clock, I thought. Before seven, she said, in La Encrucijada. Minutes passed, an hour; I worried continuously. I stayed where I was, lost, the darkness and the sound of cicadas growing all around me. A keen wind began to blow.

"Nearly eight," I said out loud.

Then another hour had gone by. Like a statue in that darkness, I stayed on; something held me there. Then it was nearly three hours, and I decided to walk the circumference of La Encrucijada. The smell of silence struck fear into me, and only the hope of finding Elena made it bearable.

I could make out a very tall outer wall topped by a chain-link fence, and nothing more. The hibiscus plants along the sidewalks were neglected and shriveled. I heard a dog barking gruffly from inside, so some sign of life. The outer wall was tall enough that the entrance, which was made of yellow glass, would have been impossible to scale.

I heard the ten o'clock train whistle by, and then some footsteps coming from behind me. I turned and saw a young woman in a black overcoat. Her smile, such melancholy in it, was striking.

"Strange to see a man around here," she said. She thrust her hands into her jacket pockets, as though her fingers might break off otherwise.

"Only a woman could bring about such a miracle," she said, her smile turning sarcastic. "Getting a man to wait out here in Témpano."

"Témpano?" I said.

"That's right."

"But this is La Encrucijada," I said. "You see that from the train before you get off."

"No," she insisted. "This is Témpano. Anyway, enough of that. Who are you waiting for?"

"Elena." I spoke the word without hesitation.

Her smile faded for a moment, and then she shrugged, before bringing a small revolver out of her pocket.

"Kill her!" she said.

"What?"

"I said to kill her! You have to. She lives in a cell in Témpano with one of Nicolás Almaraz's sons. Who sent you?"

"Elena."

"Yes, this must have been the way she planned it. It's Thursday night, isn't it? Of course—it's the only day they open the big wooden gate, and they return home in the early hours."

Then I heard a baby crying. The girl, who seemed frightened all of a sudden, said, "Keep the gun, you're going to need it. Good luck."

And with that she hurried off, as though to hide.

The baby's cries grew keener and shriller

still. They seemed to be coming from inside the town.

The cries grew louder. The echo of footsteps resounded along the cobblestones. I listened to the baby's ongoing cries. Someone seemed to be trying to soothe it now. Then, before I had time to focus my eyes, Elena appeared beneath the faint light of the streetlamps. She wore a red dress, her black hair was knotted on top, and she bore a baby in her arms, wrapped in a wool blanket.

"You shouldn't be here!" she said, clearly agitated. "We'll talk another time; I promise we will."

Tears rolled down her cheeks. Pretend tears.

"Another time!" she said. "I thought today would work, but it doesn't. They might see you, and if they do, you'll be in danger, serious danger. I'll tell you whose the baby is next time."

My heart pounded as I watched Elena disappear into the shadows around the gate's wooden surround. Anguish overcame me; I felt like the lowest of creatures. Then I remembered the gun in my hand. One bullet in the chamber.

Dry Branch

A PAIR OF BODIES DANCED naked across the dais. It was the dance for the autumn full moon, always held in the village to invoke the spirit of the *mbxü tü* bird. For hours they danced for this bird-god, weathering the cold of evening, punishing the soles of their feet until they could no longer stand. The dais, situated in the moonlit heart of the forest, was made of stone, and the priests took turns listening out for the song of the *mbxü tü.*

The dance began when the sun had set completely, and the moon became visible. The pair of dancers would mimic the movements of hunters and contort themselves to resemble trees.

And the *mbxü tü* bird did sing that night.

The dance was immediately called to a halt. According to the high priest there had been whistling followed by some birdsong that he said sounded like a snapping branch. The dancers were placed inside a bamboo cage, which was then wheeled to one of the palace's inner courtyards, and a priest said the pair would be kept there until the following day when they were to be taken to the river and thrown into the rapids. Now the dancers were afraid. Both succeeded in getting out of the cage but only the man escaped: by jumping from a window, he was able to climb away through the treetops.

The bird did not sing again. The high priest, who wore a robe of woven feathers, gave an order for the bronze gong on the watchtower to be sounded. He went over to the small stone altar, in which the clay urn of sacred swamp water was kept. Splashing his brow, he said a short prayer to the *mbxü tü* bird:

"With your song tonight, you show that

you remember us. You have not forsaken us. We pray that you put an end to the sickness that has taken so many of our men from us."

As the gong rang out across the mountain, notifying the locals, the head priest entered a trance state. He boarded up the door to the altar, opened one of the temple windows, and began intoning prayers to the forest and water spirits.

But the priest allowed curiosity to get the better of him: he decided to look at the bird. Dousing the altar fire, he put his eye up to a crack in the cane door: in the moonlight the bird was pecking at the ground around the stone dais. The rest of the priests waited in a temple passageway for the high priest to complete his interpretation of the song. It occurred to none of them that he might break with ceremonial protocol and try to look directly upon the bird.

It began beating its enormous wings. In the bright moonlight the priest saw that it had two heads, signaling the union of the gods of light and darkness. Then the bird sensed that it was being watched. With a harsh, high-pitched call it beat its wings and flew at its beholder, knocking down the door and pecking and tearing at the priest's skin.

The rest of the priests heard the shrieking.

Soon the only sound was that of the gong. The priests knew then that the bird had sacrificed the high priest. They gave an order for silence.

Moments later the bird began to call: a terrifying noise that grew louder and louder. It was like the cry of a murderer determined to go on killing. The priests went to the female dancer and forced her to dance on inside the bamboo cage. It was beyond them to know whether the epidemic would continue, or the high priest's death would be enough to put an end to the deaths that had, for so long, been decimating the village.

Bamboo Traces

I DO NOT KNOW WHY you chose to end your life, Sajuri, though I do know that if you were still here, things would have become even worse for you. The smell of your hair is with me still.

I hear the sound of patrols coming by, and the bustle of inquisitive people across from the entranceway steps. The police come, throw me to the floor, I think it's Sajuri beating me. I see them gather overhead like a dense cloud, blotting out the light from the bulb in the ceiling. Her, giving me hateful looks. Her, coming forward and thrusting a thin metal spike in my eye. I tried to shield my head. The blows from the police officers rain down, but I do not feel them. I shut my eyes, but still—her, her dismal smile. Sajuri's insane laughter resounding in my head. This should not be happening, none of it, but Sajuri is there anyway, spike in hand.

I come to. I'm in the back seat of the car, in a white body bag that is partially unzipped. Looking out, I see we are pulling up at a large quarry building. An electric door opens. The vehicle slips inside.

The food here is terrible, they've given us rice all week, though I do still welcome it; each time a bowl is placed before me I know it means I'm okay for now. I asked them to bring me the rice; then Sajuri would stop looking so angry, stop trying to get me in the eye with her spike.

Two days now I've been lying on the floor shielding my eyes. I have seen Sajuri wandering the gardens. The guards have no idea what I'm talking about, and it is better not to try to explain. Let them give me my food, that same meal, and leave it at that. I do not know why, but I have the sensation that she is watching me. It makes me so happy to see the rice dish again. My cellmates know nothing of my happiness; sometimes in the small hours I have had to hide it with bitter tears, which I know to be tears of infinite happiness. The guards on all the shifts know I request the rice dish for lunch and dinner. I ask them to put the ankle chains on me, as a sign of my willingness to comply. I have been shut off from the world, and increasingly see that this is Sajuri's doing, an ingenious way of getting rid of me. Should you not believe me, or not understand, I present the following to give a sense of the kind of person she is:

She used to leave the house early; I'd ask her to go out and find something to busy herself with. I went so far as to suggest she take a lover. She knew she was not as beautiful as she had once been, something in her eyes had dimmed forever. All I asked was that she leave me in peace. I poured myself into my painting in those days, which was my way of attaining a level of spirituality. I was becoming a solitary man; I could no longer stand Sajuri's presence in the house. An affliction began to take hold of me: all human contact was becoming unbearable to me. I asked her to leave before things got any worse. My only interaction with the outside world was via online radio stations. Conversation, talking with another human being, became completely intolerable to me.

I had nothing against her, and I told her as much; it was an aversion to people in general. Try to understand, I said.

And it was then that certain exquisite blends of color became apparent in my paintings; the kind I had always thought could only be achieved by applying oneself with great intensity. I was now free, I realized, to dive fully into my obsession with painting. I would go a whole day, two, without food, focusing my whole being on the canvas. Some critics liked what I did, but they had no idea of the suffering that went into it. Sajuri, wishing to humiliate me, began inviting people over to the house. The moment they left I would ask her to stop bringing her friends over.

Then I moved into a phase in my work when I had to commit fully to a routine if I was to progress with my painting. The process put me in touch with the sublime, and at the same time turned me into a different person.

After a couple of weeks Sajuri was back. So I began sleeping the days away and getting up around nightfall. Even just venturing onto the sidewalk opposite the house, my fearful heart would pound, I would pray to not see a soul, and a freezing wind buffeted my thoughts. I forced myself to go out like this, and when I managed it, I felt glorious. I began to think things were getting better. At one point I picked up a photo album in which Sajuri's parents appeared, and flicked through it. It was only a matter of time before I was going to be able to go out for a coffee in broad daylight.

Shortly before Sajuri left I dreamed of riding in a busy metro carriage. I shut my eyes so I would not have to see the way people were looking at me: such indifference. Some asked me where I was going. "Out!" I said. "On my own!" Then I suddenly realized that the gaze of these people was dependent on my own; if I moved my eyes, everyone around me did the same. I got off at one of the stops and the other passengers followed suit, and then they were chasing me. "Damián! Damián!" they cried. I ran all the way home, but when I opened the front door they came piling in after me. I did not know where to turn. I woke up shouting my own name.

Whenever I tried to sleep at night, I was beset by the same dream. I felt sure: if I went outside, a small slip and that would be it, people would come and chase me back to my house. I saw Sajuri everywhere, not just spying on me from windows, but even in the shower and when I went to the toilet.

It was only when I picked up my paint-brush and began mixing my colors that the great weight of that gaze—those gazes—would drop away.

A number of days later I went and found

Sajuri and tried to convince her, with every argument I could think of, to come back. I even came close to offering her money. Sajuri said I needed help, but I had no interest whatsoever in speaking to anyone. I only had to think of the questions they'd ask, the doubts they would cast on my version of events — no, I thought, not interested. Sajuri offered to go with me, but I rejected the thought outright.

I became obsessed with the idea of going to the border. It seemed to me a place where I could be totally free. I could even change my name if I wanted to, rid myself of the one they hurled at me in my dreams. The border became the subject of all my paintings. In one I had a group of children playing on the far side of a wall that still had not been completely built.

I didn't give up on the idea of going out exploring. Sometimes I would allow myself to take a couple of phone calls in a day, my heart pounding incredibly. I would say hello to whichever friend it was, tell them I had been away traveling and had just stopped by the house before heading off again in a few days. These brief exchanges were all intended to pave the way for me to disappear, at some point, for a long time. Sajuri had been gone for over a week by now. Then I answered the phone one day and it was a man asking for her. He seemed upset and could not understand who I might be, just kept insisting: "I need to see Sajuri!"

I gave him her mother's and sister's numbers.

That night, I kept hearing the man's distressed voice. What did he want Sajuri for? A few days later, I permitted myself to take two calls in a single morning. One of them was him. He couldn't find Sajuri. And he was very lonely and had decided to throw himself off the roof of his building. I could think of nothing to say, I simply listened.

After we hung up, I tried to paint a man at a window looking down at a river of people crossing the street. I tried to paint Sajuri's face as one of the passersby—lost in the welter of them. It was a small painting and I thought I would give it to the man who had been calling me.

A little before sunrise the phone rang again. I picked up and this time he said, "Are you listening? Please, I need to talk to her. I know she's your woman. She told me that herself on the snowy afternoon we were together. Every touch, every caress, she accompanied with descriptions of you. I know you're a painter. I need to talk to your woman. I have to hear her voice, just once!"

His confession was followed by tears. I tried to explain to him that Sajuri wasn't at home, and that anyway I had ended it with her.

"You're going to have to go look for her," I said.

I even tried to tell him, while being very polite, about the picture I wanted to give him, the paint of which was still wet. This time he hung up.

Days passed, and I was still consumed by the desire to make work. Along with the border, and just as mysteriously, bamboo was something I kept feeling drawn to paint.

When I was a child my father had a cabin on a bamboo plantation, on the outskirts of the city, and we would go up there on weekends. It was there that I ate bamboo soup for the first time. An aunt of ours came to the cabin and made it. I found it so delicious I knew I would never taste anything so good. Then the aunt died in a car accident. When I asked my father to make some of the soup, using tender young shoots, he forbade me to ever speak of it again; any bamboo recipe reminded him of his sister. So I made myself forget what bamboo tastes like, and only now, fleeing Sajuri's gaze, mixing my colors, does it strike me that the closest thing to the rusty yellow I have been coming up with is the hue of those tender shoots. Perhaps I should not say it, but now that I am alone and my father is dead, I have a sense that my aunt did not die in that accident. Someone told us about seeing the wreckage, and I never had cause to doubt the description, but perhaps, I now think, it was a trick on my aunt's part, a way of freeing herself from my father. I'm not sure what was the matter between them. My mother left when my brother Joshua and I were still very small, and my aunt got into the habit of joining us in the cabin some afternoons. She used to say how difficult it was to get up to the forests surrounding the city, with all those hairpins to negotiate on the road. But that morning, we were still sleeping when she arrived. I was so hungry that I woke with stomach cramps, and there my aunt was in the kitchen. And there were the bamboo shoots, out on the table, washed and chopped. She, a little annoyed, said to me, "Damián! I thought you were going to go on sleeping."

"What are you making with that?"

"Soup," she said. "It's delicious, you'll see."

My brother Joshua also died. Thinking about the bamboo stalks has enabled me to continue painting. Your name fades in the light, Sajuri. If it weren't for the smell of wet paint, which drives me on, I would be out looking for you.

Bamboo stalks have always been augurs in my life. The last time I saw my aunt, they appeared. The smell of bamboo hung about my father's coffin. I remember thinking at the time: Nobody can forbid me from talking about bamboo. The same tender shoot appears in my work now that Sajuri is gone.

Everything I produced had become a mystery to me. It was as though the canvases, full of bamboo plants, their deformed roots, their parched leaves, absorbed all bamboo plants, all roots, all parched leaves. I did not know where I was going in my painting, but the memories of Sajuri and of my father beset me once more. I lost all sense of day and night, in ecstasies as the smell of fresh paint filled my nostrils. My hands grew tired, and I began to

suffer back spasms: I knew I needed to rest. I
started taking naps out in the garden. Shutting
myself in my studio or in the living room was
not enough, I had to go out and contemplate
the night if I was to have any chance of finding peace.

"You don't know them, Joshua, so why do
you have to sacrifice yourself alongside them?
There is no garden of virgins. Think about
father, how ill he is."

What thoughts would Joshua have before
he sacrificed himself? What would prompt a
man to give his own life—and cut short the
lives of others—in pursuit of an ideal that
existed for only a handful?

"Don't do it, Joshua. Father's too unwell.
It will be the straw that breaks the camel's
back."

Now I began to understand Joshua. We
spoke together in quite an archaic way, which
was because of the other dimension he was

tuned into. Early one morning, in the waiting room of the hospital where our father was
being treated, he told me about his group's
activities, their secret meetings in safehouses.
He did not mention any names, it was just
Captain Y, Officer X. I asked him to give it
up. The Israeli-Palestinian conflict was so far
away! In our own city, I argued, there was all
kinds of violence, people being attacked, people being kidnapped.

Joshua cried bitterly that morning. Then
he reprised his old sermon about a holy war,
how there was no space for sentimentalism.
Life, he said, was nothing but a doorway to
something greater, before reciting passages
from the Koran, which he knew by heart —
passages about man giving his life to honor
God. He talked about refugee camps, about
the children being born in them, and what it
was like to grow up in such places. He knew
precisely how many of them there were and
could talk in great detail about the trials people had to endure to collect water. Does a

person who is on the verge of giving their life think of their father or brother? My brother used to spend a lot of time online, analyzing information, taking notes. He acted as though the decision were of the utmost importance. He carried a great burden, an impossibly great burden.

You could see Joshua's faith, just by looking him in the eye. One day he showed me the confirmation number for his flight, and an email which simply read: "Peace on earth."

There was a confidence in his eyes. I knew I would never see him again. It was around then that Sajuri came back for the first time, drunk, and I went on diving deeper and deeper into my solitude. Only my painting mattered. I did not know why I had refused to understand it for such a long time, but what I needed was to be alone, and to go deeply into my fears: to fall down many, many times, in order to start again.

The Priestess on the Mountain

THE GIRL SITS GAZING INTO the fire. Her hand falls on a piece of thread, she picks it up and begins making knots in it. She looks around for Yezari, her mother, who has hidden away in one of the other cells. The birth stripped Yezari of her powers of divination. Yezari's father told her about a young woman visiting these cells once, on the darkest of nights; she came in and opened all the doors, so as to look upon the inner darkness that had shaken them all so badly. Yezari is afraid to walk the hallways at full moon. Even the faintest light scares her, and she wants not to see her daughter.

The girl goes on tying the little knots. She has wavy hair like her mother. A few nights ago, near the part of the forest where people go to gather firewood, Yezari saw her daughter and felt terrified. They were so alike— excessively, almost exaggeratedly so—and there was no remedy for it now. Seeing the girl for only a few moments—she was sitting by a fire then too—brought the birth flooding back, after all these months of avoiding the memory. When the girl was born, and Yezari's gift departed, meaning she was no longer allowed to live in the proximity of the sacred swamp and the residence of the city priestesses. No longer may she walk barefoot through the main hall and feel the vibrations of the gods; a different priestess has now been charged with lighting the fire at evening, while, in Yezari's lodgings, where once she would intone prayers until deep into the night, it grows dark. One of the priests suggested she leave the city. Now she lives in one of the cells in the mountainside and goes walking in the forests as she tries to understand what has become of her connection to the gods.

Once more the moment of the birth comes back to her. The dazzling hospital lights, the pain in her belly like someone stabbing her with shards of glass. Her cries carried her up, she had the sensation of floating in a viscous substance, something she was also trapped inside.

After the cries diminished, and she felt she could bear the pain no more, Yezari came to the entrance of a tunnel. It flickered light and then dark ahead of her, as if the wiring were faulty. She hesitated, but finally decided to go on. Flickering, flashing, brilliant light, before darkness descended once more. She knew she had to keep going, and grew accustomed to the alternation of light and darkness, the silence, and the prevailing sense of peace. Suddenly she heard a child begin to cry. A terrible sound, unbearable. The light went out, the whole world lay in darkness. The doctor's voice brought her back into her body:

"It's a girl! Look, a beautiful baby girl!"

Yezari went to caress the newborn, whose

crying continued, only to find her hands covered in blood. Six months passed, more. The priests said she should go to the mountain and try to find herself once more, see if her powers might return.

The girl was already walking when Yezari saw her for the second time. The feeling of having been stripped of something sank in when she saw her daughter's face, the way she walked, the color of her hair. She had not been there to see the girl grow, she had not nursed her, had not witnessed her first words. And there she was, sitting on a park bench with Yezari's father. Harmless, like all children at that age. It was early, the girl was wearing a cotton dress. Her father had pushed her to meet the girl — she was her daughter, after all.

Yezari gave her daughter a gentle hug, and then she and the father talked about nothing in particular while the girl looked on in silence. Yezari said she had to be back at the mountain before midday and said goodbye, kissing her daughter on the forehead.

Yezari had no idea her father would then bring the girl to the mountainside. This former seer, incapable of understanding her own life. All signs were impenetrable to her now; the way the leaves moved, birdsong, none of it said anything to her about the shape of things to come. Her life resembled a gray, misty day, and she longed for the sun to break through. But then, to add to this endless murk, rains moved in.

The closer her daughter came, the more she withdrew. Hoping to recover her gifts, she began throwing corn kernels before the oracle, but they did not move and she discerned nothing in them.

The night she saw the girl sitting before the fire knotting the thread, a restless wind was blowing outside, and it weighed upon them like some kind of heavy presentiment. Yezari shut herself in her cell, covered the ground in blankets, and sat down to pray. She asked the god of water and the spirits of her ancestors to take her daughter away, that she go and be with her father again—anywhere, as long as it was far away. She did not want to see her ever again. She became increasingly lost in her prayers, and the smell of the copal sent her into a dream:

She was walking in a forest. Fear gradually filled her, and when she looked down, she found she had assumed the shape of a mountain lion.

Yezari tried to stop herself from changing, she dug her feet into the leafy ground, but as she did so claws appeared and she felt hair, a thick pelt, sprouting from her back. She hurried on and, coming to a madroño tree, decided to climb it. She cried out for help, certain that somebody, in some far-off place, was observing her transformation. The more she tried to scream, the more the screams turned to a feline mewing and yowling: *nkui nkuau, nkui nkuau.* She felt giddy and before she knew it had let go of the branch, was falling—she fell a short way, struck the next branch down, and dug her claws in to save herself. The feline noises she produced, her entreaties, eventually pro-voked the rest of the forest animals to join in. And so she knew that there was no way of flee-ing from her daughter.

When the priests found out that Yezari had turned into a mountain lion, they made an offering to the swamp gods Mbdan and Mbsiand, mixing turkey blood, white flow-ers, and the copal resin incense. The night in question was associated in the calendar with the mushroom deity, and two of the priests took a pestle and mortar out to the swamp and ground up some of the hallucinogenic fungus. They needed to find out if the girl had truly inherited her mother's gifts of foresight. The priests lit a bushel and sprinkled copal onto it, intoning their prayers to the swamp deities. "Let the words be born in the heart of Yezari's girl," they said.

They seated the girl on the grass mat and gave her a few drops of the mushroom mixture on a banana leaf. Warmth coursed through her. The priests stood in silence, waiting for her to begin speaking. Then she saw a veiled woman appear and place an ant in her hand, saying: "This red ant has cut a path to the center of the earth."

The mushrooms began to take hold, and the girl started describing the red ant and the way it frees the spirits of any person buried underground. The woman took off the dark veil and said, "I know you are looking for your mother. Her spirit has become a mountain lion and she is lost in the forest; this is what the ant has told me. This vision does not belong to you, nor does it belong to me." She sat down next to the girl on the mat. "Do you know what ferns are?"

The girl nodded.

"Where I come from, we hide our secrets in the roots of ferns. They are the only plants that go on growing in the dark."

The woman got up, covered her face once more, and walked away. The girl watched the red ant moving around her palm. When the woman was almost out of sight, she tried to get up from the mat, but something heavy held her there.

"I don't want to see Mama anymore," she said, more to herself than to the woman.

The woman could no longer hear her. She waded on through the stream that led away from the swamp. The priests heard the girl say once more, "I don't want to see Mama anymore."

Then the girl fell into a deep sleep.

The girl saw her mother, ill and alone, waiting for someone to come to her mountainside cell. She was more beautiful than the girl remembered. Her hair hung loose and there was a brightness in her eyes—the illness had not dimmed them. She was drinking a thick liquid of some kind; it had marked the corners of her mouth. She was shivering all over, as though death's cold shadow had begun to move in. She looked downcast, everything about her cried out for help, but her daughter merely said, "When you die, I will throw your body in the arroyo."

Next the girl dreamed of walking beside a stream full of beetles. This was where she would throw her mother's body, she thought. She tried to trap a beetle as it flew up into the air, but then the creature turned into a bird.

One of the priests gave an order for the girl to be taken to the temple. She, deep in her mushroom trance, was saying: "I walk in the forest, I catch butterflies, they become yellow butterflies in my hands. *Kee ꝺo'*, these butterflies are called—the voice is telling me. There is a large boulder in my path, squirrels are jumping about in the treetops. Mother, I bring you these words."

The priests encouraged the girl to continue, while dropping banana leaves on the fire to keep the evil night spirits at bay. The girl went on speaking: "A man, coming out of the misty forest. He knows his destination; you can see it in his eyes. The crows calling out, the cold ground—none of that puts him off. He carries a machete made of stone, he is using it to clear a path. He is a warrior. He hurries forward, swinging on the jungle vines to help him go quickly. Now it seems like he's flying through the trees . . . and now he's walking again. His feet kick pebbles aside, they roll away down the slopes."

When Yezari returned to her cell, she found another Yezari lying in her bed. Yezari did not know where she had been, only that she could hardly lift her arms and legs; she tried, unsuccessfully, to lift up the other Yezari, who, deep asleep, was talking: "When you die I will throw your body in the arroyo."

Yezari's body was covered in scratches. The blanket slipped off the sleeping Yezari, uncovering one of her feet—Yezari saw that they both had the same birthmark. She lay down next to the intruder and tried to go to sleep, all the while thinking about the dream of herself as a mountain lion.

•

A warrior is making his way out of the misty regions. He has been training and meditating for many days. A thick layer of cloud covers his village, and the day is dim; the yellow flowers are the only thing that seem to retain any light. This is the perfect climate for the mushrooms, and the villagers ingest them regularly. The warrior, out in the middle of his secluded area, hears the voice of the mushrooms: it calls him by his name, Lox, and says: "You must protect Yezari. Her spirit has turned into a mountain lion. If her daughter receives the gifts of foresight, she will have the ability to come to our region of mist and look into the darkness. She will do great damage to the men of our village. She is a child, there is not enough light in her heart for her to understand the peace that reigns among us."

The mushroom deity gives Lox the ability, once he enters the forest, to understand

Yezari's feline sounds: *nkui nkuau, nkui nkuau.*
He also hears what the daughter says to her
mother: "You abandoned me. I was a young
plant, I needed to grow if I was to become a
powerful tree. You went away from me, you
left me when I was still a defenseless young
shoot; when most I needed shelter, you gave
me none. You never accepted me, but the
mushrooms are merciful, and they have shown
me that something cold has filled your heart.
You walk in a forest, along a path scattered
with yellow flowers: you grow old. And your
ability to understand the gods of darkness and
light—it is mine now."

Gradually the warrior ceases to hear the
child's voice. He comes out of the forested part
of the misty region. It is cold, but his desire to
walk the path of yellow flowers is strong. He
has the sensation of many, many beetles scut-
tling all over his body, and then there is the
sound of birdsong.

The Window

YOU LOOK DOWN AT ME from your window: a group of masked men on horseback is chasing me. Mad hooves, walls of dust; I am terrified. You do nothing. One of the men, seemingly their leader, confronts me. He holds up what looks like a white handkerchief, and it has my name sewn into it. I don't know what this piece of fabric means, but I sense that it holds some significance for them. The ones behind him grow restless and dismount in one go. You carry on watching from the window; I know you won't intervene. The leader says something, but I can't understand; he speaks in a language I do not know. His words turn to shouts and his angry eyes are brimming. He throws dust in my face, half blinding me. He says something like, *"Kuanꝺ nꝺiak la"*; I have no idea what it means. He makes threatening gestures and then unsheathes his sword and attempts to stabs me. I try to run but I feel blood running down my back, and then it is between my legs, and I feel hot all over. Still you look on from your window. You turn and lie down on your bed and, in the oasis of your room, hold up the handkerchief that bears my name.

Flower María

WHEN I TOLD HIM I had been in the area for four or five days, he did not seem to understand. He could scarcely understand the happiness sweeping over me.

"This way," growled the man.

Before us was a small bamboo bridge over an arroyo of reddish stones. It was the middle of the day, and on the far side the birds, up in the branches of an annona tree, broke into song.

"Watch your step," said the man disdainfully, going first.

It was stiflingly hot. María, Flower María: as we walked, I heard the name over and over. It seemed like we were the first people to have trodden this path in years. María,

Flower María . . . *Flower María you said, you said; nothing else you said* . . . A voice echoing around inside me, a kind of torture. Then, another voice joined it, farther off: *She won't be back.* I tried to run, but someone held me back. The man was not going to let me get away.

"There's still a way to go," he said. His left eye was covered with a black scarf. A tangle of vines, broken-off bamboo leaves, and hibiscus leaves surrounded us.

"You killed her, didn't you?" said my guide over his shoulder. Before I could think of anything to say, a massive tremor shook the ground: to one side of us, a portion of the mountain was dislodged, and a landslide ensued; earth, rocks, and plants crashed across and over us.

The man screamed insults at me, calling me a reprobate, calling me snake: "We're done for!"

Above the confusion, I heard goldfinches and toucans singing out in alarm.

I came around a number of hours, or

days, later. I felt utterly weary, hungry, my body battered. No sign of the man. I remembered my brother had traveled to this region before me, and felt sure I could find him. Then I smelled copal resin smoke and came fully awake. Small rivulets of water traversed the mud. I got up and, walking a short distance, came upon a small stove with a clay griddle on top. And happiness overcame me once more: there beside the fire was Flower María.

Fingers Moving

IT WAS BECOMING HARDER AND harder
to breathe. We ran on, stumbling past spiky
ocotillo, half tripping on ferns and stubble.
My companion became exasperated by my
halting progress; I insisted on keeping to the
shadowy side of the path. In the darkness
the rotten tree stumps seemed to come alive,
and though I tried to keep going up, up, at
a decent pace, the ground kept givng way,
and I fell constantly. A certainty grew in
me, began to consume me, that we would be
devoured by the guardian spirits of the forest
we were attempting to cross so haphazardly,
so hastily. My companion shouted my name —
perhaps to check I was still there ahead of
him. He wanted to stop, said he couldn't

take it anymore. I could tell he was close to breaking, "Take it easy," I said. "Neither of us is going to die."

There was something in me, a wild animal, a kind of fury, and it would never rest. We had to stay hidden, we had to avoid being seen; otherwise I would not be able to continue testing myself. I wanted to go on, on, until I had nothing left to give. We walked a final farther stretch and I announced, "We'll stop here. This is a good lookout point."

After a few minutes the light began to fail and the sounds of night struck up, vague noises all around. Insects, protectors of the earth, shuffled along. I thought of my mission. We concealed ourselves behind the stump of an oak tree. Very quickly all we could make out were the shapes of things; I realized this wasn't in fact a good place.

"Let's carry on a ways," I said. "We're blind here."

And with that, I got up and began moving down the slope. My companion, trying to keep up, called after me, "I've got a better idea! Let's go home!"

"Home?"

He suddenly didn't care that we were being pursued? Or about the corner they had backed us into? Just like that?

"He's the one following us," I said, but it was no use. His courage had deserted him; he was not going to shoot. And yet, he stayed with me. I moved nearer to the main trail. And there was the man, coming along the path, approaching the arroyo. His white shirt, the easy gait—I knew instantly.

I imagined that, upon leaving work, two men had been watching me at a distance, and had said to each other: "How easy it would be to take out someone like this." Them, invisibly inserting themselves into my daily routine, waiting for me to leave for home, watching the way I usually went. Everything that is mine, vulnerable, exposed. Their eyes like cameras, recording every detail: the subject does not know it is being observed until the moment they pull the trigger—bang, it's all over. I imagined being on the other side of that camera, what it would feel like. This is the way these things should be done, I thought. The satisfaction flooded me, elevating me to a supramortal plane—to the level above those who are able to cut another mortal's life short.

Just then, Lisnit entered my thoughts. Her husband might find out about our relationship at any time and send someone to take me out. I felt fragile but capable of taking a life, too. My mind transmitted the signal, it passed down my arm and into my forefinger. I pulled the trigger. The man's shadow hopped, skipped over the arroyo rocks, trying to get across. Not even my companion's cries could stop the subtle movements of my fingers.

Voice of the Firefly

IT HAS BEEN FOUR DAYS since I last went out on the streets of Kelobee. A voice speaks to me, seemingly issuing from the night: "You will dream you are a small monster. I do not know if you will be allowed to go out wandering at night. People always say that the spirits are abroad at such hours, and that sometimes they resemble fireflies."

I didn't go out tonight either, I sense I will be apprehended on some corner and taken to a place where macahuite trees grow in abundance. A summary judgment will take place: I will be condemned to assume the form of a firefly. A fragile firefly that carries its light on its back. So fragile that a gentle gust of wind will one day knock it to the ground, where, among fallen leaves damp with the first rains of May, it is bound to die.

My mind is flooded with dreams. One early morning, no longer able to stand the inertia of the night, I went to my grandfather's hut.

"There's something I have to tell you," I said to him. "Someone's hunting me."

Taking me by the right arm, he checked my pulse before looking into my sleep-filled eyes—he himself looking dazed. "Go home, boy," he said. "Now is not the time."

I went home without a word. I had a feeling someone was eavesdropping on us. I checked behind the doors. All my fear came back, and a cold sweat broke out down my back. I'm not brave enough to run away from home. A terrible death awaits me outside. I have to wait until the sun comes up.

Waiting.

•

The voice again. At first it sounds very distant, like a shrieking far, far away; radio interference between stations. Then it comes nearer. And nearer, and nearer. Until the full force of its hatefulness resounds in my mind.

You needn't wait any longer.

I look around; there's no one. I shut my eyes. "Easy," I say to myself. "No one's talking to you and no one's watching you."

I go into the hallway and sit down on the floor. Cold sweat down my back again. And then the voice once more: "You needn't wait any longer!"

I go and shut myself in my room, light the candles on the candelabra, lie down on the cane bed—and then hear footsteps. Someone is approaching. Two people. They are talking: "I didn't see Hilario that night. Did you?"

It's dark, but I'd know that voice anywhere; it's so like his grandfather's.

They're talking about me. I rush to turn out the lights, but they have already seen I'm in here.

"Did you see?" one says. "The lights just went out."

"But Cástulo," says the other man in the corridor, "this boy isn't the person we're after."

Their words make me sweat even harder. The bench creaks as they get to their feet.

Then I have the nightmare about the fireflies again. I am in the fragile body of a firefly, flying through a forest of ocotillo. I try to wake, but I'm stuck. I find myself on a large rock out in the middle of a turbulent river. The sheer thundering force of the water shakes me, and I try to find a crack to gain a foothold, so that the river won't swallow me up. Impossible to believe, but there she is, in front of me; my hands rest on her hands, and I look up: it really is she.

"You, Arit?" I say, startled. "Here?"

She's in no hurry to answer. I feel the water buffeting me. A great happiness is visible in her features, it seems to overflow onto her lips. I am about to be carried away by the river, but I keep hold of her hands. She looks into my eyes. I feel her warm hands in mine.

"Come, Arit, let go of me now. You must." A broad smile appears on her face. I suddenly remember the two of us walking together: her pleading wtih me to help, to prevent her from dying of the pox. And the doctor who arrived from El Zacatal two days later, by which time she had already been buried in the village cemetery. I remember her night fevers, and bathing her using leaves from the elder plant and chigüite buds. All to ward off the pain that had been gnawing her insides, at least for a short while. But it ended up being the death of her.

"You have to let me go," I said to Arit. "You have to leave."

Harder and harder the water buffets me. I try to work myself free from her soft hands but cannot move a single finger. She's barefoot, and wears a blue dress with shoulder straps, and for a moment, dropping her head, her smile fades.

"It isn't for me," she says. "It's for Doctor Arrellanes."

Then she lets go, and in the same instant I hear someone shouting on the far side of the door: "Come out, Hilario, or we're going to torch the house."

Glancing up at the roof, which is made of palm fronds, I envisage it burning, how quickly it would go up.

I remember Arit. What it was like to touch her. My hands are still clammy with sweat.

They've been after me for days, these two. Grandfather wouldn't believe me. They're outside, they're saying my name, they say they're going to set fire to the house.

I think about Arit's words in the dream: "It isn't for me . . ."

And I know who has been after me: the doctor. It's his voice I can hear. Doctor Arrellanes. The worst kind of man — if he had bothered to hurry, Arit would still be alive. I remember the white shirt and gray blazer he wore, his jaunty look as he got down from the borrowed mule I myself had to send. We were coming back from Arit's burial when he got there. I had the black urn under my arm.

"Where's Don Nicanor?" It sounded more like a challenge than a question, but at the same time he smiled—his face revealed the patience of centuries. At his words, we halted—I and the handful of people making our way back along the single paved road through the village. He rolled up his sleeves and swept a hand back over his slick hair: "Where's Don Nicanor?"

I walked right up to him, raging.

"Don Nicanor is most likely in his house, in great anguish: his daughter died two weeks ago because our nearest doctor couldn't come in time—though he still charged us for every day he was late arriving."

Then I dropped the urn—the custom was

that it should be destroyed in church, as a way of scattering the sadness. But no. We all listened as the doctor began to laugh, a deep, guttural laugh.

"Come on!" he said. "Two thousand pesos is a fair price for expertise like mine."

He went on mopping his nape with his white handkerchief. There was no way to stop him.

The mourners just stood there, agape. I looked down at the broken urn. I turned, took the machete out of my grandfather's hand, and turned again, bringing the blade around and down on the doctor's neck. He fell to the ground. I remember the women waving their hands and screaming, but I don't remember seeing any blood: my perception was filled with nothing but the sound of the blow, as though it were echoing back off a large rock. I saw Doctor Arrellanes's face, but it was expressionless, nothing there. And a few days later I began hearing his voice. Those deep, guttural laughs again.

The men outside have gotten the fire started: I smell thick smoke spreading across the room and feel the heat from outside the door. They call for me to come out. A yellowish color fills the house, lighting up this predawn hour. I am reminded of squirrels being roasted in the hearth, a repugnant image. Fear fills me. I listen out for Doctor Arrellanes's voice, but it isn't there. I go over to the window and jump out, before making my way down to the well. Death's colors are all that I can see, they fill my vision; I am convinced Doctor Arrellanes is listening when I say: "You should not think us alike. I will pay for what I did."

Before I reach the well, I come across Grandfather, wrapped in a shawl.

"Fermín and Cástulo burned your house down," he says. "It's over, Hilario, finally it's over!"

"No, Grandfather, it isn't. I'm not like him. It will be over when I go to Zacatal and hand myself in."

I take a final look at the blazing house.

An offering—for Arit and for the doctor. My grandfather's face fills with sadness.

"El Zacatal is where this ends," I say.

The Snorting of Bulls

THE FEELING OF HIS FACE so close to mine: I couldn't stand it. Rough voice in my ear, sweaty hands on my back. It happened first thing in the morning, down at the well where the animals are watered. It was time — I couldn't stand it anymore — and I steeled myself, raised the machete, brought the machete down, slashing at his shoulder. I watched him fall to the ground between the bulls' hooves. The perplexed look on his face. He tried to say something, but even if he had managed to, I wouldn't have been able to hear: I had struck down the man I was most afraid of — the reason I often refused to go down to the fields — and yet now my terror was even greater.

He lay in his own blood, mumbling something. The sticky red started to coalesce with the dust in the sweltering heat of morning.

My feet felt pinned to the ground, and my hands refused to move. I thought of returning home, but now didn't know which way to go. Aquileo was dying between the clumps of long grass. His voice petered out. I felt something running against my feet; his blood was forming a pool around them in the dust.

The bulls wheezed drily. Taking in the smell of the fresh blood, perhaps. Aquileo lay completely still. He must be dead by now, I thought, and with that his death began to weigh on me. I couldn't remember where I'd dropped the machete. I searched along the path, which brought me out in front of the well. I plunged my feet into the water, but it was like I had plunged them into still more blood. An asphyxiating heat had sprung up inside me—like I had drunk strong liquor. I felt unsteady as a wooden doll. My feet and my head were not part of me, they felt like those of a giant. My hands, tiny and useless.

When I got home I found my grandfather eating his lunch by the fire.

"Girl," he said, still looking at his food. "Why so long out there?"

He told me to eat something.

"No, Grandfather. I don't feel well, I need to rest."

Suddenly the heat inside me gave way to piercing cold. I lay down on a mat, pulling some thick blankets on top of myself. My grandfather came over. Eating a tortilla, he ran his hand across my forehead.

"Girl, you have a fever. A bath in tea leaves for you."

I heard a voice out in the passageway. The cold seemed to lock around my toes. I heard my grandfather arguing with someone.

"Impossible," he said. "My girl has a fever, she's burning up."

"We've come to take her."

Voices—more than one. I saw shadows moving between the cracks in the guarambo enclosure. Then shouting, then I couldn't hear my grandfather's voice. A number of men I did not know entered the house. Fury in their eyes. The youngest of them ripped the covers off me, and I became a block of ice, unable to move. The oldest of the men spoke:

"The whole village knows."

I felt as though a fistful of snow had been shoved into my mouth. I said nothing to any of their questions. I heard the bulls snorting while the younger men set about kicking me, before the others dragged me, bed mat and all, out into the passageway. Then I saw them raise their sticks and begin bringing them down— on me, or the block of ice I had now become. I tried to tell the older man that the bulls were coming, that they'd be here at any second, but couldn't get the words out, couldn't be heard. When they came thundering in, they flattened the guarambo like it was paper. The men turned and ran in terror, but were mostly trampled. I saw the frothing mouth of the lead bull. Then other noises, here, there, before I finally passed out.

When I came to, a number of hours later, my grandfather was dabbing my forehead with a washcloth soaked in salt water.

"Aquileo didn't die, he's just badly wounded. You left him crippled."

Our hut was still thick with the smell of the bulls, but the guarambos were still in their place.

PERGENTINO JOSÉ RUIZ was born in 1981 in a Zapotec village in the Pacific highlands of Oaxaca. He has published poetry and prose in both Zapotec and Spanish, and is a member of the Sistema Nacional de Creadores de Arte, the Mexican government's prestigious fellowship program for artists and writers. He has a Master's in Hispano-American Literature from the Universidad Austral de Chile. He has been a fellow of Fonca (2005), the Fondo Estatal para la Cultura y las Artes de Oaxaca (2008), and the Ford Foundation (2011–2013). He was included in the México20 anthology of the best Mexican fiction writers under forty, which was published in English (Pushkin Press) and in Spanish (Malpaso).

THOMAS BUNSTEAD was born in London in 1983 and currently lives in west Wales. He has translated some of the leading Spanish-language writers working today, including Agustín Fernández Mallo, Maria Gainza, and Enrique Vila-Matas, and his own writing has appeared in publications such as *The TLS*, *Brixton Review of Books*, *LitHub*, and *The White Review*.

Thank you all
for your support.
We do this for you,
and could not do
it without you.

PARTNERS

AVAILABLE NOW FROM DEEP VELLUM

FORTHCOMING FROM DEEP VELLUM

AMANG · *Raised by Wolves*
translated by Steve Bradbury · TAIWAN

MARIO BELLATIN · *Mrs. Murakami's Garden*
translated by Heather Cleary · MEXICO

MAGDA CARNECI · *FEM*
translated by Sean Cotter · ROMANIA

MIRCEA CĂRTĂRESCU · *Solenoid*
translated by Sean Cotter · ROMANIA

MATHILDE CLARK · *Lone Star*
translated by Martin Aitken · DENMARK

LOGEN CURE · *Welcome to Midland: Poems* · USA

PETER DIMOCK · *Daybook from Sheep Meadow* · USA

CLAUDIA ULLOA DONOSO · *Little Bird*, translated by Lily Meyer · PERU/NORWAY

LEYLÂ ERBIL · *A Strange Woman*
translated by Nermin Menemencioğlu · TURKEY

ROSS FARRAR · *Ross Sings Cheree & the Animated Dark: Poems* · USA

FERNANDA GARCIA LAU · *Out of the Cage*
translated by Will Vanderhyden · ARGENTINA

ANNE GARRÉTA · *In/concrete*
translated by Emma Ramadan · FRANCE

GOETHE · *Faust, Part One*
translated by Zsuzsanna Ozsváth and Frederick Turner · GERMANY

PERGENTINO JOSÉ · *Red Ants: Stories*
translated by Tom Bunstead and the author · MEXICO

JUNG YOUNG MOON · *Arriving in a Thick Fog*
translated by Mah Eunji and Jeffrey Karvonen · SOUTH KOREA

TAISIA KITAISKAIA · *The Nightgown & Other Poems* · USA

DMITRY LIPSKEROV · *The Tool and the Butterflies*
translated by Reilly Costigan-Humes & Isaac Stackhouse Wheeler · RUSSIA

FISTON MWANZA MUJILA · *The Villain's Dance*, translated by Roland Glasser ·
The River in the Belly: Selected Poems, translated by Bret Maney · DEMOCRATIC
REPUBLIC OF CONGO

GORAN PETROVIĆ · *At the Lucky Hand, aka The Sixty-Nine Drawers*
translated by Peter Agnone · SERBIA

LUDMILLA PETRUSHEVSKAYA · *Kidnapped: A Crime Story*, translated by Marian
Schwartz ·
The New Adventures of Helen: Magical Tales, translated by Jane Bugaeva · RUSSIA

JULIE POOLE · *Bright Specimen: Poems from the Texas Herbarium* · USA

MANON STEFAN ROS · *The Blue Book of Nebo* · WALES

ETHAN RUTHERFORD · *Farthest South & Other Stories* · USA

MUSTAFA STITOU · *Two Half Faces*
translated by David Colmer · NETHERLANDS

BOB TRAMMELL · *The Origins of the Avant-Garde in Dallas & Other Stories* · USA